I'D RATHER
BE EATEN BY
SHARKS

I'D RATHER BE EATEN BY SHARKS

BY ELAINE MOORE

ILLUSTRATED BY LORI SAVASTANO

A
LITTLE APPLE
PAPERBACK

Love to Green
Elaine Moore

SCHOLASTIC INC.
New York Toronto London Auckland Sydney

ISBN 0-590-47918-0

12 11 10 9 8 7 6 5 4 3   6 7 8 9/9 0/0

Printed in the U.S.A.   40

First Scholastic printing, February 1995

For Ellen, Joanne, and Eva

Contents

1. A Strange Houseguest   1
2. Anyone for Acapulco?   12
3. Where's Chester?   23
4. In the Library   29
5. A Stinky Case of Stage Fright
   and a Bit of Bad Luck   44
6. Joy Speaks Up   54
7. Speaking of Pigs   62
8. The Important Thing   77

I'D RATHER
BE EATEN BY
SHARKS

1

A Strange Houseguest

"A pig?" Dad asked. "Please pass the peas," he said.

Joy waited. She knew what would happen next. Seated across from her at the supper table, her silly sixteen-year-old brother, Harry, was hunched over his plate. Before Mom could stop him, he made a low snorting noise. Joy covered her mouth with her napkin and tried hard not to giggle.

"A pig?" Dad said again. "Here? In this house?"

What Joy's father meant was that River

Bend Estates, where they lived, wasn't exactly a farm.

"Darling," Mom answered, smooth as silk. At the same time, she passed Dad the peas. "Even if Chester wasn't an adorable little potbelly pig . . . even if he was the biggest porker on the face of this earth . . . I had no choice."

Harry looked at Joy and winked. Harry was in high school and had a lot of friends who did neat things like build gigantic floats for the spring festival. This year they were making a Viking warship out of chicken wire and toilet paper. A pig at home fit right in with the rest of Harry's outrageous life as a high school junior.

Joy took a deep breath and waited.

Mom was an attorney. Like Harry, she thrived on the unusual. For two weeks now, all Mom had talked about was the custody battle over a precious little pig. Personally, Joy had wondered how anybody could like a pig enough to fight over him. A dog that fetched balls or a white horse with a long swishing tail, Joy could see. But what could a pig do except oink?

Even so, Mom's new client, the very rich Mrs. McRadisson, was suing her millionaire ex-husband, Mac McRadisson, for thirteen million dollars and a potbelly pig. Joy thought Mrs. McRadisson ought to have her head examined. It was too much. But Joy's mother believed that the real reason she succeeded where other lawyers failed was because she always went the extra mile for her clients. And now she had taken in this pig!

Joy could only imagine what her father would say about that.

Joy's father was a pilot. When he came home on Friday nights, he liked everything to be the same. Joy did, too. But it rarely was.

"Why, just look at him, dear," Mom went on, still talking about the pig. "He's already at home here sleeping in front of the TV just the way you do after a long trip. Why don't you just think of Chester as a house-guest?"

Mom was too smart to wait for an answer. Instead she turned to Joy.

"Sweetheart," Mom said, "why don't you tell us what happened today in school."

Joy closed her eyes and took a deep breath.

"I have to give a spoken report to the whole class."

As far as Joy could tell, no one else in third grade was bothered by the assignment Miss Merry gave the class last Monday. No one else thought they might throw up or faint when they had to stand up and say something in front of the whole class.

"Probably you haven't thought about it like this before," Miss Merry told the class, "but you've been giving speeches all your life. The first time you asked your mom for a cookie, that was a speech."

"What about when we went for an increase in our allowance?" Billy Maroney wanted to know. Billy sat in the front row. He had red hair and more freckles than Joy would ever want to count. He also had a purple tongue from chewing grape bubble gum and green eyes he liked to cross whenever anyone looked at him. He was a regular walking, talking rainbow.

"We'll start by thinking of things we might want to talk about," Miss Merry went on. "Billy has already suggested one idea. I'll expect to see ideas on paper from each of you in my idea box tomorrow morning. On Wednesday we'll begin by visiting the library. Then you'll write your outlines and move on to working on your speeches. You'll see. It'll be fun!"

Somehow, Joy didn't believe the fun part. How could throwing up and fainting in public be fun?

"If you're stumped, boys and girls," Miss Merry suggested before taking them to the library on Wednesday, "you might want to talk about something you did during your vacation."

Using the special black-and-silver airplane pen her father had given her, Joy bent over her paper and wrote the only word she could think of. *Acapulco*. As far as Joy knew, the only reason her family went to that special vacation place in Mexico during spring break was because her father got free plane tickets.

By Friday afternoon, Joy was getting worried. All she had on her paper were three words:

Acapulco. Acapulco. Acapulco.

That afternoon, shortly before dismissal, Miss Merry crooked her little finger in Joy's direction. With teeny tiny steps, Joy slowly made her way to Miss Merry's desk.

"You haven't handed in your assignment," Miss Merry whispered. "We need to talk."

Behind her, Joy heard the kids stuffing their knapsacks.

"Joy, you are one of my nicest, brightest, and most generous students," Miss Merry went on as she rose up off her chair. "And your vacation sounds so interesting.

" 'Acapulco, Acapulco, Acapulco.' Why, I've always wanted to go there. And you've been to Acapulco so many times. Your family must love it or why else would you go? You need to tell us. What did you do? Did you snorkel? I'll bet you brought a whole suitcase back filled with coral and pretty shells. Surely you'd like to share some of your experiences with your friends?"

Joy felt Miss Merry slowly turning her about so she'd face the class. Joy felt Miss Merry's hand gently raise her chin so she'd stop staring at her sneakers. When Joy looked up, Billy Maroney crossed his green eyes and stuck out his purple tongue.

Not counting herself, there were twenty-eight kids in Joy's class. That made fifty-four regular eyes, two crossed green eyes, and one fat purple tongue. They would all be looking at her while she was supposed

7

to remember what she was supposed to say. It would be the same way her whole family was looking at her now.

How could Joy not be scared?

"Sweetheart?" Mom's voice brought her back to the supper table. "Had you thought what you might talk about?"

"No, I don't have the slightest idea," Joy whispered. Mom and Dad were looking at her with anxious expressions. Not Harry. He was grinning from ear to ear as he motioned with his head toward Chester.

Awake from his nap, Chester was sitting in his basket, looking like a gray fuzz ball. His pointed face turned back and forth, up and down. His beady eyes searched the room. He wasn't missing a thing!

"He might be scared," Harry whispered.

"Probably doesn't know where he is," Mom whispered back. "He's just a little pig, not even three months old. You can see why Mrs. McRadisson wants custody."

"Of course," Dad said as Chester's snout wrinkled in the funniest way.

"What's he going to do now?" Joy asked.

Chester's pointed ears pricked forward. He stood up and swished his tail. He rocked back and forth.

"He's trying to make up his mind," Joy said.

Then with a squeaky grunting noise, Chester trotted quickly toward the table on his four skinny legs.

Dad was first to chuckle, then Mom. Soon they were all laughing. They laughed even harder when Chester sat down beside Joy's chair, a smile stretching across his cute little face.

"Ever since I read *Charlotte's Web*, I have always wanted to have an intelligent pig!" Joy said, sliding onto the floor to hug him.

Without being told, Chester hopped into Joy's lap. He pressed his cold snout against her hand. Then he rested his prickly gray head on her leg and began making strange contented-sounding noises.

Joy stroked Chester's prickly gray fur and smiled. This sure was some pig!

Gosh, she thought quietly to herself. Just wait till I tell Amanda. I bet I'm the only kid at Flint Hill Elementary who has an intelligent pig for a houseguest.

2
Anyone for Acapulco?

Joy could think of a million better things to do on such a beautiful Saturday morning than write a dumb speech that was going to make her throw up in public, but "First things first," Mom always said. "Homework comes first." It was just another secret of Mom's success she was only too happy to share with her daughter, Joy.

Joy sat on her bed and stared at the blank piece of paper in front of her. Then she glanced at the little gray pig sleeping in the pile of laundry she'd tossed on the floor.

Except for the few times he'd gotten up to get a drink of water in the kitchen and to use the litter box in the bathroom, Chester had slept there all night. Joy smiled to herself. It felt a little funny sharing a room with a pig, but he wasn't messy and he didn't smell or anything. Then Joy went back to working on her speech.

A half hour later, Joy was still staring at the paper. It had taken awhile, but she'd finally written a title.

Acapulco.

Now all she had to do was find something to say.

Joy chewed on her pencil. Maybe she could recite the scary shark poem Harry had told her on the beach.

The thing about sharks is teeth.
One row above and one row beneath.

Just then, the bedroom door popped open and Mom stuck her head inside. Joy almost screamed. For a moment she thought it was "Jaws."

"Joy, baby. I have to run to the office. Be a dear and watch Chester, will you? You know I can't rely on Harry. Your father and I think he may have parked his brain on that monstrous Viking ship the junior class is building for the spring festival. I can't ask your father, either. He's had to take the skis in to The Chalet to be repaired."

Mom took a deep breath. "You remember when your father ran over the prickly holly bush in Vail? It messed up the tips. You know we can't procrastinate on these things, Joy. It's like I always tell you and Harry, if you attend to the details, the major points will take care of themselves. If your dad doesn't take care of the ski tips today, he's liable to end up with two broken legs next season. You know they'd never permit him to fly with his legs in a cast. So if you could just watch Chester for me. It's an absolute emergency.

Dire. You understand, don't you, sweetie?"

Joy grimaced. "Sure."

Lucky Mom. She got to work in an exciting office while Joy was stuck doing a boring dumb speech that was going to make her throw up in front of her whole class.

"I'll help you when I get back," Mom added, sounding guilty. "I've been thinking of some good topics you can cover. We want a forceful presentation, don't we, sweetie? We do want that A, don't we?"

Joy listened as the front door slammed. Chester snored lightly in his sleep. Every once in a while, his body shook as if he were having a dream.

Joy went back to her speech.

Harry was the next to interrupt.

"Tell Mom I'm through studying. I'm going over to the Liberts' to work on the float. We're just about finished wiring the horn to the battery." Harry cupped his broad hands around his mouth and bellowed like a Viking warrior.

"Hey!" Joy covered her ears.

"Sorry. Actually, the horn's about a million decibels louder than that, but you get the drift. Oh, yeah," Harry said as he started to leave. "I almost forgot. Tell Mom I'll be home for dinner. She doesn't have to call the Liberts. I won't be late."

Joy shook her head. Everyone knew Harry was never on time for anything. Dad said it started when Harry was born. Most babies show up after nine months. Harry took almost ten.

Now her big brother had left her all alone in the house with Chester. Joy felt more responsible than ever. It was her job to protect the little pig.

Like, what if Mr. McRadisson sent a bunch of ferocious thugs in black ski masks with only their eyes showing, armed with guns and gunnysacks, to pignap his little darling? Mom would kill her if anything happened to Chester.

Joy went from window to window, upstairs and downstairs, making sure that everything was locked. Then she checked the back doors, the garage door, the basement door, and the door to the attic. She checked the front door to make sure Harry had locked it behind him when he left.

Joy was meticulously punching the buttons on the alarm system when she heard the first peculiar noise followed by a funny thud, rumble, rumble, thud, thud, followed by a pig's snort and a grunt.

Joy raced for the kitchen. She skidded across the tile in her sock feet. The lower cabinet was open wide when Joy knew for a fact it was closed a few minutes ago. Then she saw Chester!

Chester was rolling potatoes across the floor with his snout.

"Chester! How did you do that?" Joy shut the cabinet.

Right away, Chester stepped forward. Before Joy could stop him, the little pig curled his snout around the handle of the cabinet.

"You'd better not do that again!" Joy

warned. For emphasis, she tapped her toe the way Mom sometimes did.

Chester didn't seem to care! He answered with a stubborn-sounding grunt, then pulled the door open again!

Great! Joy thought. I'll never get my speech done now. Then she remembered how Mom had said Mrs. McRadisson trained the little pig with raisins.

Feeling desperate, Joy pulled a raisin out of one of the boxes Mom sometimes put in her school lunch. She held the raisin in front of Chester's snout. Then she closed the cabinet door and tapped Chester on the snout with her finger.

"No," she said firmly.

When Chester backed off, Joy gave him the raisin. Chester eyed the cabinet suspiciously. Then he looked at Joy. Finally, Chester turned around and stalked out of the kitchen, swishing his tail as cool as could be.

"C'mon, Chester," Joy called as she

headed back up the steps to her bedroom. "As smart as you are, you can help me with my speech."

Joy cleared some paper off the bed and sat down. Even with Chester there in her big house with her, for the first time in a long while, Joy wished they all were in Acapulco. Even with the windows and doors locked, even with the alarm system on, empty house noises gave her the creeps.

When the phone rang, Joy jumped.

"Gosh, Amanda. I was sitting here all by myself," she said, breathless. "You shouldn't call me like that. You scared me to death."

"Don't be silly. How would I know you were alone? Besides, I wanted to read you my speech. It's about the family reunion we had last summer. Wait till I get to the part about the babies. They were so cute."

Joy had seen pictures of Amanda's baby cousins at least a million times. They all looked like Amanda. They all had curly hair and bangs.

Joy lay back on her bed. She tried not to fall asleep as Amanda read her speech over the phone.

"Do you like it?" Amanda said at last.

"Yeah, it's um . . . it's um . . ." Joy struggled to think of a better word than boring. "It's very restful," she said finally.

"Well, nobody got much rest with those babies. But we did rest a lot on the way home. What are you doing your report on? Oh, yeah, Acapulco. We've been there. Don't tell me, I want to be surprised."

Joy knew better. What Amanda meant was she'd been to Acapulco at least a million times. Anything Joy had to say would be restful — except Amanda would say dull and boring instead. Joy pictured her classmates sitting in front of her while she talked about Acapulco. Everyone would be snoring. Except Billy Maroney. He would be sticking out his purple tongue. It was enough to make Joy want to throw up.

"Look, I have to go now," Joy told Amanda. "I want to finish my report. I'm just getting to the good part.

"What am I going to do, Chester?" she asked once she'd hung up. "Miss Merry's going to be so disappointed and Mom's going to kill me."

Joy scratched Chester behind the ears with her pencil. Suddenly, she broke into a smile that felt like the sun coming out after a storm.

"Hey, I can talk about you, Chester! It will be just like I said last night after dinner. Ever since I read *Charlotte's Web,* I've always wanted to have an intelligent pig."

Then Joy shook her head in despair. "Gosh, Chester. The only problem is, except for you, I don't know anything about pigs. And my speech is due Monday!"

3
Where's Chester?

"What's going on? Who reset the alarm? Joy! Are you upstairs? Where is everybody?"

Mom always asked a lot of questions when she came home. Harry said it was because their mother spent so much time in court where everyone asked everyone a bunch of questions. Mom was like a leaky faucet. She didn't know how to turn the questions off.

Joy hurried down the stairs and into the den.

"I stopped by the travel agency for information on Acapulco," Mom said as she unloaded stacks of brochures from her briefcase. "Here are some pink index cards for your notes. Everything is organized in my head. I did it on the way home in the car."

Joy took a tiny step backwards. She shifted her weight to her other leg.

"Um, Mom." Joy's hands fidgeted nervously. "I changed my mind. I thought maybe I could tell the kids about Chester."

"Chester?" Mom's eyes widened in surprise. She wasn't smiling. "But I already did all this work. I even told our travel agent that I'd bring your report in for them to review. They want to use it for some promotional material. You know, what every kid should know about Acapulco. Just imagine how that will look on your resume. You'll be eight years old and already published. All the information is here. Joy, just look at this stack of . . ."

Joy hadn't heard Dad come in, but she

could feel his hands resting comfortably on her shoulders.

"Can't the promotional people do their own piece?" Dad said to Mom. He cleared his throat before continuing. "It sounds to me like the beaches in Acapulco are playing second fiddle to your houseguest."

"But, darling, Joy doesn't have any material. It's Saturday. Late!" Mom tapped her watch nervously with her fingernail. "How do you expect Joy to get an A if she starts a big project like this at the last minute?"

"Whoa!" Dad said. "I thought we paid for a new library with last year's tax increase. You'd think they would have something on potbelly pigs."

"Speaking of pigs," Mom said, ignoring Dad and turning to Joy instead, "where is Chester?"

"I just saw him a minute ago," Joy said. "He was lying beside my bed reading Harry's comics. I mean, it *looked* like he was reading Harry's comics."

"Well, I haven't seen him!" Mom sounded frantic. "Where is he? Chester! Chester!" Mom hurried from room to room but Chester was nowhere to be found.

"Come out, come out, wherever you are!" Joy tried, remembering that Mrs. McRadisson had said that Chester liked to play games just like a child.

"Maybe he got out," Dad said, joining in on the search. "Did Harry leave the door open? You know Harry has never closed a door in his life."

"Don't even suggest it!" Mom was getting hyper. "Nothing moves as fast as that pig. He could have easily scooted out when the door was open. Honestly, Joy, I told you to watch Chester and not let him escape. Do you think for a minute I want the entire staff at Arnold, Finnegan, Porter, and Mays laughing at me? Not only that, the McRadissons would sue us over that pig! This is terrible!"

Joy had more important things to worry about.

"I can't believe it! Mom, Dad! My speech has disappeared into thin air." Joy raised her arms and let them flop to her sides in desperation. Nobody was paying attention.

She turned on her heels and started back through the house. "Chester! Where are you, Chester?"

For the third time, Joy checked her room. She looked under her bed. She sorted through the laundry. She even picked up her robe and shook it, not that Chester could have hidden in the folds, but she had to be sure. She looked on top of her bed. And then she noticed her pillow was moving.

That's funny, Joy thought. I only have two pillows and now there's three.

That's when she noticed the third pillow was Chester.

Chester must have crawled inside the pillowcase, a nice cool little cave. When he couldn't back out, he'd gone to sleep.

After all, according to Mrs. McRadisson, Chester was just a baby.

Gently, Joy slipped the pillowcase off the little pig.

"Well, now," Dad said as Chester licked Joy's face with his tiny pink tongue. "I'd say we have here the topic for a very interesting speech."

4
In the Library

Joy could hardly wait for Monday. She would know more about pigs than anybody. It was like she had a secret. As Joy sat in the front seat of the Volvo, she could hardly keep quiet. She wasn't scared at all.

The only thing that had her even the tiniest bit nervous was worrying that Dad might get lost. Joy toyed anxiously with the zipper on her jacket. The library closed at six o'clock. That only left tomorrow for writing her speech and for Mom to type her notes on those pink index cards she'd brought home from the office. Joy only had this one chance to get as much information as she possibly could on pigs. The problem was it took Dad longer than it should to find the library.

"Why don't you ask someone," Joy said finally. "You could ask at the gas station. That's what Mom does."

"I never ask directions." Dad peered at the dry cleaners opening up across the street. "I might go in circles but I always find my way."

"What about up there?"

Dad looked where Joy pointed.

"Where?"

"In the sky. When you're flying your airplane. Do you get lost up there?"

"Pilots fly," Dad said matter-of-factly. "They don't steer. The steering is done on the ground."

Joy stuck her fists firmly into the pockets of her red jacket and took a deep breath. What a terrifying thought. Good thing she wasn't giving a speech about that. The next time someone had a trip to take they wouldn't go by plane.

"Whoa!" With a screech of the wheels, Dad zoomed the Volvo across the line, over the speed bump, and into the library parking lot.

"You drive like Harry. Bumpy," Joy told Dad as she climbed out of the Volvo.

Harry was a lot like Dad. When Harry got lost, he never asked for directions, either.

A few minutes later, Dad was ushering Joy through the library's heavy glass doors. Joy's stomach did a quick flip-flop. Most of the round wooden tables were already taken.

What if she had to sit at a table with someone she didn't know? Worse, what if she had to sit at a table with someone she *did* know?

Joy pulled at her father's sweater. She was going to tell Dad how she'd changed her mind, how she'd talk about Acapulco instead, how she'd use all those great brochures Mom brought home from the office and how she didn't need to research in the library after all, when Dad found a table that was empty. He plopped Joy's knapsack on the table and opened it up.

"We'll go to the card file first," he said in a loud voice.

"Shhh!" Joy put a finger to her lips, at the same time looking both ways to be sure there was no one in the library she knew.

"We'll want to see if they have anything on potbellies."

Joy cringed. Did he really have to say that word? Saying "pigs" was bad enough. Did he have to say "potbellies"?

"I think this library has computers," Joy whispered. She hoped Dad would take the hint and keep his voice low.

He didn't.

"Good." Dad's voice echoed. "Good to see my tax dollars put to good use. Let's see if they have anything in the computers about . . ." Joy winced as he said it again. ". . . potbellies."

"I'll wait here by the table so no one else takes it," Joy whispered meekly. No one should know she was with the man who was looking for potbellies.

When Dad came back, he was carrying an armload of books. "All you have to do is read these." He stacked them in a huge pile where Joy was sitting. "This is going to be some speech. Of course, Mom and I will help. We'll have a dress rehearsal tomorrow evening. I'll make a tape with the camcorder. That way you can watch yourself."

Behind the stack of books, Joy struggled to keep from trembling. A tape? Watch herself? Throwing up in front of Billy Maroney would be lots easier.

Dad opened the book on the top of the stack. "Here, read this on pork barrels. We don't want to leave any stone unturned. Pets, pork, there's even a section in the data base on Vietnamese pig farming. You stay here. I'm going back for more."

Dad was too much. If she wasn't careful, he would have her reading every book in the entire library.

Joy struggled to lift the heavy pork barrel book off the top of the stack. Just then she saw someone she would recognize anywhere. Sitting at the next table, his back to her, was Billy Maroney. Nobody but Billy Maroney had hair as red as that.

Joy's breath caught. How long had Billy been there? Had he seen her come in? Maybe not. Maybe as long as he didn't turn around, as long as he didn't get out of his chair, as long as he didn't look in her direction, she would be safe.

But what if he did. What if he saw her?

Joy's heart pounded in her ears. Her skin turned clammy.

Maybe, Joy thought, she could pull her shirt up over her head. Maybe he wouldn't recognize her without her head showing. Joy took hold of her shirt with both hands. That was when she thought of something else. If she pulled her shirt up, her belly button would show. That would be worse.

There was only one thing she could do.

Quickly, Joy slipped her arms out of her jacket. Then she pulled her jacket up so the collar rested on the top of her head like a crown and the arms hung down like long red ears. It was like wearing a tent.

Joy was sitting under her jacket when her father came back with an armload of books.

"Joy, what are you doing?"

"I'm being invisible. Can't you tell? Anyhow, this is how I study. Haven't you ever seen me study like this before?"

Joy snatched a piece of paper and slipped it inside her jacket tent. If only she'd brought her flashlight. Or a fan. Next time Mom took her to Nordstrom's to buy a jacket, she was going to ask for a jacket that was air conditioned.

"Perhaps I can help?" Joy heard a muffled voice that sounded very kindly.

Joy turned so she could see through the narrow slit in her tent. The voice belonged to a lady librarian. Probably, Joy thought, there was a law against reading so many

pig books all at the same time.

"We're doing a report on potbellies," Joy heard Dad say proudly.

"Pigs," Joy whispered. "Little pigs."

"Oh, my!" the librarian exclaimed. "What a fascinating subject. Perhaps we should check the periodical index. That's where we can find a listing of all the magazine articles that have been written about your little pigs. You can pick what's most current or what interests you the most. And, if we're lucky, we'll even have the magazines in this library for you to look at today."

"Can we take the magazines home?" Joy wanted to know.

"You can't check out all the magazines but you're welcome to make copies on our copier."

"It's not exactly a report," Joy said. "It's more like a speech."

"Then you definitely want to find the most current information on the subject." The librarian held out her hand. "Let's check the periodical index together."

Still wearing her red tent, Joy reached through the slit and took the librarian's hand. Behind them, Dad boomed, "I'm good with copiers. I have a whole roll of dimes. Just point me in the right direction."

"You know what's funny?" Joy told Mom that evening at the dinner table. "The more I read about pigs, the more I want to know. The more I know, the more I want to talk about it."

"Yes, sweetie," Mom said, "and by the time I decipher those snippets of paper you and your father crammed into your knapsack and am ready to start typing your index cards, you'll be ready to begin working from your notes. How long is your speech supposed to be?"

"Three minutes," Joy said.

"We might have a rough time keeping it to three minutes. You have so much material to draw from. You don't suppose Miss

Merry would allow you to expand on your speech somewhat, do you?"

"Hey," Harry interrupted before Joy had a chance to respond. "Sorry I'm late."

He took a chair and straddled it. "We got hung up on the float. You should see it, Mom, Dad." Harry turned to Joy. "It's the biggest, most stupendous Viking boat around." When Harry flung out his arms, Dad grabbed for the milk. "Got a hull the size of ten elephants," Harry boasted. "It's almost a half a block long." He turned back to his mother. "If we don't win the trophy for best float at the festival, I'd say the contest is rigged."

Dad waited a minute before tapping his coffee cup with his spoon.

"I was about to say, Harry, that tomorrow night we're making a video of Joy's speech. We'll expect you to be here and on time."

"A dress rehearsal in the living room," Mom added in case Harry didn't understand. "You are to be here, cheering your sister on. That's what families are for. You can tell your friends," Mom added. "No phone calls after seven o'clock. Joy is going to get an A on her report and all of us are going to help."

By Sunday afternoon, Chester was a comfortable member of the family. He ate his pig meals in the kitchen. He lapped the water out of his plastic bowl and used the kitty litter box faithfully. All without being told. Pigs are really, really smart.

When Joy wasn't looking, Chester crawled under her bed and walked away with a sock. After that, Chester wanted to explore everything. He even tried to get in the shower with Dad.

"Honey, why don't you take Chester for a walk," Mom suggested after she opened the dishwasher and Chester sniffed inside.

Chester answered with a happy-sounding grunt. A pig's happy grunt is one of the nicest sounds. The next thing Joy knew, she and Chester were strolling down Maple Avenue.

"Is that a pig?" a woman called from her car window.

"Yes, it is," Joy said proudly as she stepped off the curb, expecting Chester to follow across the street. Chester didn't. Instead, he got halfway across, took one look at the woman's car, and stopped dead in his tracks.

Poor terrified Chester! His squeal could have broken eardrums. Most people don't know, Joy thought to herself, but if you're not careful, pigs could make you deaf.

Joy coached Chester forward with a raisin. "Pigs don't like to be picked up," she explained to the startled driver. "They like to keep their feet on the ground. Pigs used to be wild animals. Their enemies would snatch them up by the back of the neck and shake them."

Joy felt proud of all she had learned about pigs. And so was her family that night when Joy gave her report as her

father ran the camcorder. If only she could show the video in class instead of having to do the whole thing live.

That night, Joy tossed and turned, thinking about all the terrible things that were going to happen when Miss Merry called on her the next day.

5
A Stinky Case
of Stage Fright and
a Bit of Bad Luck

Joy was sitting at her desk and minding her own business when she saw Billy Maroney turn around to tell Nicholas about the alien he'd spotted in the library over the weekend.

"It was about the size of a small midget," he said, loud enough for anyone to hear. "And it was wearing a red jacket."

Joy was trying to decide where she could bury her jacket when Miss Merry turned away from the chalkboard.

"Boys and girls, I want you to put your

subtraction trees away now. Take out your speech notes so we can begin sharing our reports. When I call your name, I want you to come to the front of the class." Miss Merry's eyes grew round as she smiled. "Can anybody guess what I want the rest of you to do? I'll give you a hint. Call it out, class. A good audience pays . . ."

"Attention!"

"That's right. They listen to what is being said. And I want all of you to be a very good audience. Just like I'm going to be a very good audience from the back of the room."

As Miss Merry walked between the tables, she stooped to pick a grape gum ball off the floor beside Billy Maroney's desk.

Everyone started taking out their notes. Joy's were typed neatly on big pink index cards. Sitting next to Joy, Amanda giggled as Billy pulled out a rumpled paper with scribbles and a big purple spot that smelled like grape.

Joy tried not to notice.

What was happening? Why was her stomach doing strange things? Just then, oh yuk! Down the hall, the cafeteria workers were cooking up a batch of greasy green beans for lunch. The smell traveled into the classroom like a pukey green cloud floating through the air. Joy pinched her nose tight and scooted down in her chair.

"Joy, that's not necessary. Amanda, would you like to go first?"

Whew!

Any other time, Joy would have worried. She wouldn't want Miss Merry to think she was rude.

Joy let go of her nose as Amanda made a beeline to the front in her new patent leather shoes and ruffled red socks. Her speech was clipped inside a blue folder, the kind big kids use. Amanda stood beside Miss Merry's desk. She opened her folder and blinked.

Billy Maroney blinked back. He crossed his eyes.

"We have about a zillion new babies in

our family," Amanda began. "Well, not a zillion exactly, but we do have a lot."

Right away, Billy made a baby's face. *Waaaa waaaaaa.* He scrinched up his face like he was starting to cry. Then he did a stupid thing with his fingers. He was going to suck his thumb!

Amanda didn't seem to mind.

When Amanda got to the part about being an aunt even though she was only eight years old, Joy slid the red rubber band off her index cards. Pigs were more interesting than babies any day.

Joy waited until Amanda told about the zillion baby playpens at her family reunion. Then Joy flipped the first pink card over and read it quietly to herself.

> Ever since I read *Charlotte's Web*, I have always wanted an intelligent pig.

Joy flipped to the second card, the third, and the fourth.

Pigs are smarter than you think. They like to watch TV and read the comics.

So far so good. As Amanda rattled on about burps and bottles, Joy recalled everything she was going to say about pigs.

Pigs have a soft spot behind their ears. They like to be tickled there.

Pigs eat pig meal. They're very neat and tidy. They aren't messy. They make lots of neat noises, but the best is that pigs have handy snouts — not just for what you'd think like sniffing and snorting. They use them to wake you by pulling the covers off your bed. They also use them to open kitchen cabinets and roll potatoes around on the floor. But potbelly pigs are hardly any trouble because they are smart and easily trained.

Joy was going to tell how she trained Chester with raisins.

Suddenly everyone in class was clapping. Joy glanced around just in time to see Amanda heading back to her chair, a smug look on her face.

That was when Joy noticed. Her foot had gone to sleep! Joy tried to shake it awake. Miss Merry might call on her! What if she tripped and fell? Everyone would laugh. Then she would *have* to faint. Or, maybe she could have a heart attack.

Very carefully Joy eased her foot back under the table. She shook it very quietly. Joy kept her shoulders down. She imagined Miss Merry in the back of the room craning her neck as she checked out all the tables. Maybe she would call someone else next.

"Nicholas. I have a feeling you have a very interesting report to share with us today. How about it?"

Everyone was paying attention as Nicholas shuffled to the front of the room. He was grinning shyly to himself as if whatever he said was going to be good. Billy Maroney cleared his throat. Then Nicholas turned around, looked up at the ceiling, took a deep breath, and began to tell about the worms he was keeping in a box in his backyard.

"Ooooh, gross. No fair," someone said as Billy Maroney put his hands to his throat as if he was being strangled by a giant worm and was going to puke. Next, Billy made his finger look like a worm wriggling across the table! When his finger got next to Amanda, he stuck out his purple tongue.

Nicholas didn't notice. Neither did Miss Merry in the back of the room. Probably she had better things to do.

Joy flipped to the next card.

Pigs are full of mischief. They can also be very stubborn.

"Joy. Joy! JOY!"
From somewhere far away, it sounded

like Miss Merry was calling her name.

Oh my gosh, she was!

Joy heard but she couldn't move. Her hands were mushy wet snowballs. Her foot was pins and needles. The greasy green bean smell from the cafeteria was ten thousand times worse. Joy stood up and tried to walk but her knees kept caving in. Then, the worst — Billy Maroney turned around and smiled his crooked smile.

Finally, somehow — Joy didn't know how — she made it to the front of the room. And Joy stood there, holding on to the cards.

I have always wanted an intelligent pig, Joy said to herself. I have always wanted . . .

Joy opened her mouth and shut it.

Amanda was drawing pictures on her report cover.

Nicholas was tearing his speech into bits and rolling them into spitballs.

And then Billy Maroney did what Joy knew he would do. He crossed his green eyes and stuck out his purple tongue.

But Joy wasn't going to be scared. Not even when she saw the fifty-four regular eyes all looking at her.

Joy took a deep breath. "Ever since I read *Charlotte's Web* . . ."

"Can you speak a little louder, Joy?" Miss Merry said in her special way. "We . . . your friends in the back row want to hear you."

Joy swallowed. She glanced at the clock. Maybe there would be an earthquake in the next five seconds. Joy felt herself start to sway.

"Ever since I read . . . I have always wanted . . ."

"Yes, Joy. You have always wanted . . ."

"An intelligent pig," Joy blurted louder than she meant to.

At the same time Billy Maroney made a loud snorting noise. He pushed his nose up with his fingers and kept it there. A pig face.

"Miss Merry," Joy thought she whispered. But if she did, Miss Merry didn't hear. Joy wanted Miss Merry to tell Billy how he was not a good audience, but she didn't. And right away, Joy forgot everything else she was ever going to say. Joy just stood there. Not one single word came out of her mouth.

There was no earthquake. The floor didn't swallow her whole. Joy didn't faint. Thankfully, Joy didn't throw up. All that happened was a loud bell started to ring inside of Joy's head.

What was happening?

Chairs fell to the floor with a bang as kids jumped to their feet. Miss Merry slammed the windows shut. Everyone lined up at the door. Where were they going? And what was that loud ringing noise that sounded like . . . ?

Oh, no! Joy groaned. A fire drill.

6

Joy Speaks Up

"Of course, you'll have a second chance to-morrow," Mom said at dinner. Great! Just what Joy wanted to hear.

"We know how much preparation you put into your speech, sweetie. You had all those cards and they were all typed so nice and neat. Isn't that so, Frank?"

"Joy was ready," Dad answered. "Sounds like a bit of bad luck to me. Tomorrow will be better."

Across the table, Harry winked.

"But, Mom," Joy said, trying to explain.

"Even if the bell hadn't rung . . ."

"Darling, I don't think you understand. Miss Merry will give you a second chance. The fire drill wasn't your fault. All you have to do is give the speech tomorrow. She'll call on you first. After a good night's sleep, you'll be fresh and ready to go. C'mon, let's look in your closet. We'll pick out something bright and fun to wear."

Mom pushed back her chair, ready to bolt up the stairs. "Didn't Grandma send you red ruffle socks last Christmas?"

Groan. "No, Mom. Red ruffle socks won't help."

"What do you mean they won't help?"

"It won't. The problem was, I forgot."

"You forgot?" Mom stared at Joy. "But you rarely forget anything. Harry, on the other hand, would forget his head if it weren't attached to his neck. What is it you think you forgot?"

Joy said, "I forgot what I was supposed to say."

That was the last thing Mom wanted to

hear. "After I went to the travel agent and got all that information on Acapulco? After you changed your mind and decided to talk about a pig? After I spent the whole weekend deciphering your notes and typing them on index cards?"

Dad reached over to pat Joy's hand. "When you rehearsed in front of Mommy, Harry, and me, you were wonderful. I have everything on tape."

Joy nodded sadly. "But today I wasn't wonderful."

Mom frowned. "You didn't forget the cards?"

"I had the cards," Joy stammered. "They didn't work. I mean, they did at first, but then when I stood up and my stomach rumbled and . . ."

"To tell the truth," Dad mused out loud. "I wondered about those cards. I never use index cards when I give a speech."

"There you go again," Mom said, putting down her fork. "And what do you use, Frank? I suppose you use a road map."

Mom threw back her head, laughing at her own joke.

"As a matter of fact," Dad answered smoothly, "the last time I addressed the National Conference of Air Traffic Controllers I did use a road map. I stood in the convention hall in front of twenty-five hundred people with a *road map* and did just peachy."

"Peachy. I never heard of anything so crazy. A man who flies around with his head in the clouds using a road map?"

Ignoring Mom, Dad turned to his daughter. "Joy, come on around here where you can see."

Joy watched Dad unfold a paper napkin. He took his pen out of his pocket. Joy waited politely until Dad was finished. Then she shook her head sadly.

"You draw good pigs and I like your road map, but I don't think even that's going to help," she said.

"I know!" Harry shouted. "What if you had a prop? What if I used my tape recorder and got a tape of Chester grunting? Hey, I could do it in stereo. Then all you'd have to do is set your boom box on Miss Merry's desk, turn it on, and snort, snort, grunt, grunt, you have . . ."

"Harry!" Mom cut him off. "Don't be silly. Your sister is not taking pig grunts into her classroom!"

"No," Joy announced, feeling suddenly very cool and collected. "I'm going to take the real thing. I'm going to take Chester."

"Take Chester!" Mom said. "That's impossible. Pigs don't belong in school."

"Mom!" In case she wasn't listening, Joy pulled on her mother's arm.

Meanwhile, hearing his name, Chester scurried through the living room as fast as his skinny legs could carry him.

"Mom," Joy repeated as Chester took his usual place on the floor beside her chair. "Harry's right! Last night for dress rehearsal, I had Chester. I did a good job. Even you said I did. You clapped and everything."

"Yes, darling, you did a wonderful job. That's why I can't understand . . ." Mom sounded flustered. "Joy, there are rules! Your principal will never allow a pig in your classroom."

"But Mom, you always talk about setting precedents with your law cases. Chester will just have to be a precedent because I want Chester to be my prop."

"The principal will never give permission."

"She will if you call Miss Merry. Besides," Joy continued, "it'll be good experience for Chester. What if you need to use Chester as a witness in court? After being in my classroom, he'll know how to behave in a crowded courtroom."

Harry patted Joy on the back.

"All you have to do is call Miss Merry." Joy reminded her as she handed Mom the cordless phone.

Across the table, Dad winked at Mom and smiled.

*　　*　　*

"I know it's silly," Mom said a few minutes later. "I never expected Joy's teacher to cave in so easily. I was so sure she'd refuse that I never stopped to think how we would get Chester to her school."

"What about a limousine?" Harry suggested.

"Can't you bring him, Mom?" Joy asked quietly.

Joy watched as her mother's shoulders rose and fell. "Oh, honey, I would," she said in a sad and truthful way. "I really would but I have a court date tomorrow. I couldn't let my client down."

She stopped to glance across the table. "But your father . . . he might . . ."

Joy didn't wait for Mom to finish.

"Daddy!"

Dad put both hands up. "Whoa! I'm flying the shuttle to Boston. I won't be back until late."

On the floor beside her chair, Chester made a pig noise that sounded like Harry. Joy looked at her brother hopefully.

"Harry?"

"Hey. No sweat." Harry's chest puffed out. He smiled broadly.

"You?" Mom sounded stunned. "But . . . but . . . I won't have you missing school for a pig. Harry, you have college to think of. You know, it's never a good idea to cut class. . . ."

Harry waved her off. "Me, cut a class? Hey, Mom! That would never happen. Don't worry, folks. Like I said, no sweat. I'll get the dainty little pig to Joy's school and I won't even have to cut a class to do it."

Joy was afraid to ask how.

7

Speaking of Pigs

"Don't worry," Harry reassured Joy the next morning when she woke him up a little earlier than usual.

Harry yawned and turned over on the mattress. His face was still wrinkled with sleep.

"I'll take care of everything," he mumbled. "When do you give your speech? Two o'clock?"

"Harry, I told you last night! One o'clock! We go to lunch at twelve. After that it's

restrooms and recess. Write it down, Harry. Please."

Joy waited while Harry sat on the edge of his bed and rummaged around on his nightstand for a pencil and paper.

"What did you write down, Harry? Read it back," Joy said, afraid that Harry might be sleeping now.

Harry yawned again. "Restrooms . . . recess . . ."

"Not that part," Joy screamed. "Write down one o'clock! Are you awake, Harry? Really awake?"

"Yeah. I mean, no. Um." Harry yawned again, this time louder and longer than before. Or was it a snore?

"Harry?"

Sometimes, like right now, having Harry for a brother could be awfully difficult.

"Gotcha," Harry said after a long wait. "Chester will be at your school at twelve fifty-five on the dot. Oh. Wait a second. I almost forgot. Joy?"

"Harry, you're scaring me."

"What school do you go to? Is it the one on the hill?"

"No, Harry. That's the high school. *Your* school. My school is at the bottom of the hill. It has a flagpole in front."

"Gotcha. Bottom of the hill. Flagpole. Restrooms and recess. Don't worry," he said again. "I'll be there."

That's what Joy was remembering as she sat at her desk after lunch, after restrooms, and recess. Just three little words. *I'll be there. I'll be there.* By now her stomach had turned completely upside down. She looked up at the clock. Twelve forty-seven. *I'll be there.*

It was like waiting for an execution. Hers.

Joy tried repeating the words Miss Merry said would help.

"I like to share with my friends. I like to share with my friends." Joy glanced around the classroom. "These are my . . ."

Just then, Billy Maroney turned around

in his chair, and, looking straight at Joy, crossed his two green eyes and stuck out his fat purple tongue.

It was twelve forty-nine.

Joy squeezed her toes inside of her shoes. Now at least she didn't feel sick to her stomach. She was just worried Harry wouldn't show up with Chester.

Twelve fifty-two. Joy twisted in her seat to peek out the window. The only thing out front was the flagpole.

Twelve fifty-three. Miss Merry was wearing an expectant look on her face. Joy answered it with a shrug.

At the same time, Joy tried to remember all the places that had flagpoles. Was Harry at the post office? Or the sheriff's office? He wouldn't have gone to the White House, would he? What would the President want with a pig? Or would Harry stop to think about that?

Joy wondered if Miss Merry had a number she could call.

"Hello, Mr. President, is there a silly

brother there with an intelligent pig?"

Twelve fifty-four.

At twelve fifty-four and a half, Miss Merry glanced at the clock, smiled at Joy, and raised her eyebrows. Joy knew what Miss Merry was thinking.

Where was Chester?

At one o'clock, Miss Merry motioned to Joy.

"Class," she said, "put your books away. Clear your desks. We want to pay good attention now as we resume our talks. Joy will be first."

As Joy walked to the front of the room, she could feel her classmates' eyes on her back. Just in case Harry didn't make it, Joy had brought the pig pictures Dad copied at the library. She also had a small box of raisins in a brown paper bag. Pictures and raisins weren't exactly the real thing but as props they would do fine.

These are my friends, Joy reminded herself as she set her road map on the lectern. She put the props on Miss Merry's desk.

Joy glanced around the room and searched for a friendly face. Bravely, she tried to smile. Joy opened her mouth to begin her speech but instead of words, she heard a horrible, loud, and ferocious noise.

Oh, no! Not again! The blaring noise grew louder and louder. Whatever it was, it was coming closer to the school!

Joy shook her head in disbelief. It couldn't be! A Viking horn? Not even Harry would be that silly.

Standing beside Miss Merry's desk, Joy was close enough to the window to peek outside just in time to see Harry and his friends park their gigantic Viking warship in the school driveway. There in the bow of the ship, the sun shining on his silver helmet, stood Harry. Right beside him, happy as could be and wearing dark sunglasses, sat Chester.

Joy watched, her heart pumping madly, as Harry climbed down off the float and took Chester's leash.

At the same time, Billy Maroney ran to the window.

"Hey, there's a Viking pig out there! It just got off a Viking warship and it's coming inside!"

By now the whole class was crowding the window. Miss Merry was calling for everyone to sit down. No one cared.

Down the hall, Joy heard the kids in the other classes hollering. Everyone had seen Chester dressed in his red bandana and dark sunglasses, his tail swishing as he walked daintily up the steps and through the front door of the school.

A few minutes later, Miss Merry motioned Joy into the hallway.

"Chester!" Joy cried happily.

Wiggling and snorting, Chester pawed at Joy's shoes with his cute little feet. Joy didn't care who saw. She got down on the floor so Chester could poke her with his damp snout and lick her with his tiny pink tongue. She hugged him and let him make happy sounds into her shirt.

Joy was too busy scratching Chester's soft tummy and saying hello to pay attention to what Miss Merry was whispering to Harry. But before she knew it, Miss Merry's hand was on Joy's shoulder and she was walking Joy and Chester up the aisle to the front of the class.

Slowly, they turned around. "Class, I'll take my place in the back of the room again. Remember to show Joy and your guests your best manners."

Joy watched Miss Merry move to sit beside Harry. She guessed Chester was watching, too, because he tugged slightly on his leash. Probably, Joy thought, Chester doesn't like being in the front of the room any more than I do.

Feeling sorry, Joy knelt down to give Chester another pat. It wasn't fair that Chester should be scared, too.

"There, is that better?" Joy said softly, slipping the sunglasses off his snout. She unsnapped his leash and straightened his bandana.

Behind her the kids were whispering in their seats.

"Is it trained?" Amanda asked.

"Don't be silly," Billy Maroney answered. "You can't train a pig."

Too busy to care, Chester was looking off to the side and sizing up Miss Merry's desk. When Joy caught him eyeing the teacher's chair, she knew what would happen next.

Sure enough, Chester trotted over, and with one light jump, bounded into Miss Merry's chair. He put two feet up on her desk and grabbed the apple off the top.

"Chester," Joy reminded him while everyone else laughed. "Miss Merry said to show our best manners. She meant you, too!"

Startled, Chester looked at Joy and blinked. The wrinkles in his forehead deepened. Then, setting the apple down on the desk where it belonged, Chester turned his head left and right as he surveyed the third-grade classroom.

"These are my friends," Joy said by way of introduction.

"Wow, I'm impressed," Billy Maroney said loudly as he snapped his fingers at the little pig.

"Hey! Watch out!" someone screamed as Chester leapt from his chair and raced toward Billy Maroney as fast as his little pig legs could carry him.

"Get away! Shoo! Shoo!"

Billy fanned his arms but Chester wouldn't stop. He rooted in Billy's desk until a whole bag of purple gum balls rolled onto the floor, one by one.

Billy tried crawling after the gum balls that were rolling all over the place. Finally, Billy sat back on his heels.

When he did, Chester poked his snout into Billy's pocket and pulled out a gum ball.

"No fair. What is this? A trick pig?"

"No," Joy answered matter-of-factly, "Chester is just your ordinary run-of-the-mill average potbelly pig."

Joy looked up at the rest of the class. "You see, pigs are very smart. They are smarter than poodles. They are smarter than ponies. Only monkeys and dolphins are smarter than pigs."

"No fooling," Nicholas said. "They ought to use pigs for drug busts."

From the back of the room, Miss Merry cleared her throat.

"Perhaps this would be a good time to begin your speech, Joy."

Joy signaled to Chester and, right away, he jumped into Miss Merry's chair and sat down.

Then, after glancing at her cards, Joy began her speech. Halfway through, she noticed something strange.

Billy's arms were resting on the table as he leaned forward. He didn't want to miss a word she was saying.

Amanda wasn't doodling.

Nicholas was paying attention, too.

In fact, everyone was paying attention. Except for the sound of her voice, there was not a noise in the room. Joy glanced over at Chester whose head was cocked in the cutest way. Even Chester was paying attention to her.

Joy was a flower starting to bloom — and bloom and bloom until suddenly she felt very important. And she kept feeling important until she'd finished her speech.

"Does anyone have any questions?" Joy asked. "If so, I'll do my best to answer."

For a moment, the old fears returned. What if no one raised their hand? What if no one cared? Then, the most amazing thing happened.

Billy Maroney clapped his hands. Nicholas was next. Before Joy knew it, the entire classroom — including Miss Merry and Harry — burst into applause.

8
The Important Thing

To celebrate Joy's success, Dad offered to take everyone out to dinner at a fancy restaurant with white tablecloths and waiters with white napkins on their arms. Except for the clinking of silverware and glasses, the restaurant was almost as quiet as the library.

They had already told the waiter what they wanted to eat. Joy sat back in her chair. Now that her speech was over, she was surprised how relaxed she felt.

She was hoping Harry remembered his

manners. She hoped he didn't stretch his mouth with two fingers and stick his tongue in and out like a gila monster. She hoped he didn't make her giggle when she was drinking her milk.

Joy waited politely for the lull in her parents' conversation that would surely come.

"Why was I scared?" she asked Mom as soon as there was a chance.

Mom patted Joy on the leg and smiled. "Everyone gets nervous when they give a speech. Not just kids. Grownups get nervous, too. Even successful lawyers like me."

"Wow." Joy blinked. She could hardly believe it.

"The important thing, sweetie, is that you handled that nervousness. You gave an outstanding speech, Joy, and you are to be commended for it. Even if you did use a pig for a prop."

From the lighthearted way Mom said it, and the way Mom winked at Dad, Joy knew she was teasing.

"At first," Joy said, "I thought, well, if Harry doesn't come, I still have my other props. I would have been OK. But when Harry did come with Chester, that was the best."

Dad leaned forward and cleared his throat. "We're still not sure," he said. "Exactly how did Harry get to your school?"

Harry was busy chewing his bread, so Joy answered for him.

"Well. Harry had to do his float for the spring festival. The teachers had to be sure the floats wouldn't conk out so they had a rehearsal parade. With the floats. Harry just took a little detour. And he DIDN'T cut class."

She was careful to emphasize the last in case Harry was about to get into trouble.

"Some detour," Dad mumbled into his napkin.

"But, it was for some PIG, remember?"

And with that said, Joy winked at her brother.

About the Author

When a person has two different jobs, we say that the person "wears two hats." Elaine Moore wears two hats. She's a writer and a speaker. As a speaker, she actually *does* wear a hat — a bright purple baseball cap. She wears the cap when she goes out to visit schools as an author in residence. No wonder she's known by children across the country as "the lady in the purple hat."

Even though Mrs. Moore is used to speaking in public, she admits to occasional stage fright. How does she overcome it? She follows her own good advice — the same words of wisdom that Miss Merry tells Joy in this story: Think of the audience as your friends.

Elaine Moore is the author of *Sarah with an H*, a Little Apple paperback published in 1992. She's also written several hardcover picture books. *Grandma's Promise* and *Mixed-up Sam* were IRA/CBC Children's Choice books.

Mrs. Moore lives in Great Falls, Virginia.